D0232448

OLIVER
AND AMANDA'S
HALLOWEEN

Jean Van Leeuwen

PICTURES BY

ANN SCHWENINGER

DIAL BOOKS FOR YOUNG READERS
NEW YORK

To David
(the ghost, gorilla, Batman, pirate)
and Elizabeth
(the princess, rabbit, Raggedy Ann, clown)

J.V. L.

For Lloyd

A.S.

Published by Dial Books for Young Readers
A Division of Penguin Books USA Inc.
375 Hudson Street
New York, New York 10014

Library of Congress Cataloging in Publication Data
Van Leeuwen, Jean.
Oliver and Amanda's Halloween
Jean Van Leeuwen ; pictures by Ann Schweninger—1st ed.
p.   cm.
Summary: Oliver and Amanda Pig's Halloween activities include
making their costumes, getting a pumpkin for a jack-o'-lantern,
and going trick-or-treating.
ISBN 0-8037-1237-5 — ISBN 0-8037-1238-3 (lib. bdg.)
[1. Halloween—Fiction. 2. Pigs—Fiction.
3. Brothers and sisters—Fiction]
I. Schweninger, Ann, ill. II. Title.
PZ7.V32730mh 1992   [E]—dc20   91-30941   CIP   AC

First Edition
1 3 5 7 9 10 8 6 4 2

The full-color artwork was prepared using carbon pencil,
colored pencils, and watercolor washes. It was then scanner-separated and
reproduced as red, blue, yellow, and black halftones.

Reading Level 2.0

CONTENTS

DRESSING UP

"What should we be for Halloween?"

asked Amanda.

"I don't know," said Oliver.

They looked in the dress-up box.

Oliver pulled out two masks.

"Let's be spooky monsters!" he said.

"That's too scary," said Amanda.

She pulled out Father's bathrobe.

"I know what," she said.

"You can be a king

and I will be a princess

and we can wear gold crowns."

"Yuck!" said Oliver.

He pulled out a tall hat.

"I know what," he said.

"You can be a witch

and I will be a mean black cat."

"Witches are scary too," said Amanda.

"We could be ballet dancers

and dress up in this lace tablecloth."

"We could be ghosts," said Oliver,

"and dress up in white sheets."

"How about being a mother and father?"

said Amanda.

"Sally Rabbit can be our baby."

"How about being skeletons?"

said Oliver. "We can paint bones

on our old pajamas."

"I've told you and told you,"

said Amanda,

"I don't want to be something scary."

"Amanda's scared of skeletons

and ghosts and spooky monsters!"

said Oliver.

"I am not," said Amanda.

"I just don't want to be one."

"Fine," said Oliver.

"I'll be a spooky monster

and you can be a dumb princess."

"Fine," said Amanda.

Oliver reached into the dress-up box.

Way at the bottom
was Father's nightshirt
and Mother's funny flower hat
and Oliver's magic glasses.
Oliver put them on.

"What do I look like?" he asked.

"A creature from outer space,"

said Amanda.

"Really?" said Oliver.

Amanda put on Mother's ruffled blouse

and Father's fishing boots

and a cooking pot on her head.

They looked in the mirror.

"We are pigs from another planet,"

said Amanda.

"That's it!" said Oliver.

"That's what we'll be for Halloween."

THE PUMPKIN

In Father's garden

a pumpkin was growing.

All summer it had been getting bigger

and fatter and rounder.

Now it was ready to pick.

On the day before Halloween
Oliver and Amanda and Father
went to the garden.

"Wow!" said Oliver. "That is
the biggest pumpkin I ever saw."
"It is the biggest one I ever grew,"
said Father.
"It's as big as me," said Amanda.

"I will carry it," said Oliver.

He tried to lift the pumpkin.

"You can help me, Amanda," he said.

Oliver and Amanda pushed.

They pulled.

They fell down.

But the pumpkin would not move.

"This job calls for a wheelbarrow,"
said Father.

The three of them lifted the pumpkin
into the wheelbarrow
and wheeled it to the kitchen.

"My oh my," said Mother.
"I could make that pumpkin
into a lot of pies."

"We are going to make it
into a jack-o'-lantern," said Amanda.
They lifted it onto the kitchen table.
Father began to carve.
First he cut a round hole on top.

Oliver and Amanda took out the seeds.

"Ugh!" said Amanda. "They're all wet."

"Why are there so many?"

asked Oliver.

"So we can toast some for a snack,"

said Mother.

"And plant more pumpkins,"

said Father.

Father began to cut out the eyes.

"What kind of face

should our pumpkin have?" he asked.

"A mean scary face," said Oliver.

"No!" said Amanda. "A happy face."

"Halloween is supposed to be scary, you know," said Oliver.

"But not too scary," said Amanda.

"I know what we can do," said Father.

"Amanda, you tell me
what kind of eyes to make."

"Round happy eyes," said Amanda.

"Oliver, you tell me about the nose."

"Long and crooked," said Oliver,

"with a wart on the end."

Father did the eyes and nose.

"Now for the mouth," he said.

"Smiling," said Amanda.

"Frowning," said Oliver.

Father carved a mouth that went up
at one end and down at the other.

"Make lots of teeth," said Amanda.

"Not teeth," said Oliver. "Fangs."

Father made teeth on the bottom
and fangs on top.

"There," he said.

"Our jack-o'-lantern is finished."

Mother put a candle inside.

"It looks kind of scary," said Oliver.

"And kind of happy," said Amanda.

Father smiled.

"Then it is just right," he said.

DONUTS

"Trick or treat!" said Amanda.

"Give me something good to eat."

"Stop saying that," said Oliver.

"I'm just practicing," said Amanda.

It was Halloween.

The jack-o'-lantern

was in the window.

Oliver and Amanda were waiting

for it to get dark outside

so they could go trick-or-treating.

"Is it almost dark yet?" asked Oliver.

"Not yet," said Mother.

"Come and help me make donuts."

Oliver and Amanda cut out the donuts.

Mother cooked them.

She let Oliver and Amanda

eat the holes.

They stacked donuts on plates.

They piled them on platters.

"Why are there so many donuts?"

asked Amanda.

"So we can give one to everyone

who comes to our door," said Mother.

Mother put the donuts on a high shelf.

"Now is it almost dark?"

asked Oliver.

"Not quite yet," said Mother.

Oliver and Amanda put on

their costumes anyway.

They walked around the house,

waiting for it to get dark.

Oliver sniffed.

"Those donuts smell good," he said.

"Yes," said Amanda. "Anyone

who comes to our house is lucky."

Oliver looked up at the donuts.
"Twenty-five, twenty-six,

twenty-seven," he counted.

"I bet Mother won't need that many."

"Oliver," said Amanda,

"you can't have those donuts."

"I just want one," said Oliver.

"How can I go trick-or-treating

when I am weak and hungry?"

Oliver climbed up on a stool.

"You better not," said Amanda.

Oliver climbed on top of the counter.

"Mother will be mad," said Amanda.

Oliver climbed up on the refrigerator.

He stood on his toes
and reached for a donut.

"Watch out!" said Amanda.

CRASH! The plate toppled over.

It fell on top of Oliver.

Oliver fell on top of Amanda.

Donuts went rolling.

Mother came running.

"Are you all right?" she asked.

"No," said Amanda.

"I am all squashed."

Mother picked her up

and kissed all the places that hurt.

"I only wanted a donut," said Oliver.

"You could have asked," said Mother.

"Now you will have to clean up

this big mess."

Oliver cleaned up all the donuts.

Amanda's hurts got better.

She looked out the window.

"Guess what?" she said.

"It's dark outside."

"Oh boy!" said Oliver.

"Time for trick-or-treating."

THE MONSTER

"Good-bye," said Mother.

"Have fun!" said Father.

Oliver and Amanda walked down

the road, carrying their pumpkins.

"We are going to get zillions

of candy bars," said Oliver.

"And cookies and apples and donuts.

I hope we get lollipops."

Amanda did not say anything.

She was looking at the dark.

It was so black

and full of spooky shadows.

Suddenly Amanda saw a monster
at the side of the road.
It was big. It had ten hairy arms.

"What's that?" she whispered.
"It's only a bush," Oliver said.
Amanda looked again.
The hairy arms were just branches.

They walked up to a house
and knocked on the door.
Someone opened it.
"You can say it now," said Oliver.
"Trick or treat! Give us something
good to eat," said Amanda.

"Oh boy!" said Oliver. "Lollipops!"

At the next house they got apples.

At the next house they got cookies.

Oliver and Amanda kept walking.

Suddenly Amanda saw a monster

coming toward them.

It had horns, a long tail,

and horrible fangs.

With it were a ghost and a skeleton.

"I'm scared," squeaked Amanda.

"Hi, Oliver," said the monster.

"Hi, Bernard," said Oliver.

"And Rosie and James.

These are my friends, Amanda."

Amanda looked again.

The horrible fangs were just a mask.

The long tail was a rope.

"Nice costume," said Amanda.

"See you tomorrow," said Oliver.

They went to four more houses
and then they started home.

On the way Oliver counted his candy.
"I got three lollipops," he said,
"two Crunchy-Munch bars, jelly beans,
and all those apples and cookies."
Suddenly Amanda saw a monster
in front of their own house.

It had a huge head

with awful staring eyes,

a lot of teeth, and a terrible smile.

And no body.

"Help!" cried Amanda.

"It's a real monster!" yelled Oliver.

"Get me out of here!"

Amanda tried to run

but she tripped over her boots

and fell down.

Any second now

the monster was going to get her.

"Wait a minute," said Amanda.

"Pigs from another planet

aren't afraid of a little earth monster."

Suddenly she felt brave.

She peeked at the monster again.

"Why, it's only our jack-o'-lantern!"

she said.

"I knew it all the time," said Oliver.

Mother and Father were standing

in the doorway.

"Did you have fun?" asked Father.

"I got three lollipops," said Oliver.

"I saw three monsters," said Amanda.

"But they weren't real."

"How about a donut?" asked Mother.

"Trick or treat!" said Amanda.

"Give us something good to eat."

940078

E
Van   Van Leeuwen, Jean
ABC
                 Oliver and Aman-
                 da's Halloween

DUE DATE

940078